Come Here, Tiger!

Come Here, Tiger!

Alex Moran

Illustrated by Lisa Campbell Ernst

Green Light Readers
Harcourt, Inc.
Orlando Austin New York San Diego London

Come here, Tiger.

Where is that cat?

Is that cat in the bed?

No, it's Scotty!

Come here, Tiger.
Is that cat in the box?

No, it's Rabbit!

Come here, Tiger.
Is that cat in the tub?

No, it's Frog!

Come here, Tiger.
Is that cat in the hat?

No, it's Turtle!

Come here, Tiger.
Where are you, Tiger?

Look! Here you are!

Oh Where, Oh Where

The girl in the story looked all over for her cat, Tiger.

Sing "Oh Where, Oh Where Has My Little Dog Gone?" Use the word **cat** instead of **dog**.

Has My Little Cat Gone?

Oh where, oh where has my little cat gone?

Oh where, oh where can he be?

With his ears cut short and his tail cut long,

Oh where, oh where can he be?

A Book Full of Pets

The girl in the story loved her cat, Tiger. What are your favorite pets?

WHAT YOU'LL NEED

- paper
- crayons or markers
- tape
- pencil
- stapler

1. Think about one of your favorite pets.

2. Draw a picture of the animal.

3. On another piece of paper, write the things you like about the animal. Tell why you would like to have that kind of pet.

4. When you are done, tape the two pieces of paper together.

I like fish.
They swim.
They are pretty
to watch.

I love dogs.
They play with you and
they are good friends.
My dog licks my
face all the time.

5. Think of other pets you like.
Draw pictures and write about them, too.

6. When you are done, make a cover
and staple all of the pages together.
Now you have your own book full
of pets!

My
Book
of Pets

Meet the Illustrator

Lisa Campbell Ernst loves to illustrate books about animals. Before she painted the pictures for *Come Here, Tiger!* she thought about her own pets. They became the models for the animals in this story. And Lisa Campbell Ernst's daughter was the model for the girl who is looking for Tiger!

© Vedros & Associates

Lisa Campbell Ernst

www.HarcourtBooks.com

First Green Light Readers edition 2001
Green Light Readers is a trademark of Harcourt, Inc., registered in the United States of America and/or other jurisdictions.

The Library of Congress has cataloged an earlier edition as follows:
Moran, Alex.
Come here, Tiger!/by Alex Moran; illustrated by Lisa Campbell Ernst.
p. cm.
"Green Light Readers."
Summary: A little girl encounters various animals before finding her cat.
[1. Cats—Fiction. 2. Lost and found possessions—Fiction.]
I. Ernst, Lisa Campbell, ill. II. Title. III. Green Light reader.
PZ7.M788193Co 2001
[E]—dc21   00-9726
ISBN 978-0-15-204820-4
ISBN 978-0-15-204860-0 (pb)

LEO 10 9 8 7
4500247470

Ages 4-6
Grades: K-1
Guided Reading Level: B
Reading Recovery Level: 4

Green Light Readers
For the reader who's ready to GO!

Five Tips to Help Your Child Become a Great Reader

1. Get involved. Reading aloud to and with your child is just as important as encouraging your child to read independently.

2. Be curious. Ask questions about what your child is reading.

3. Make reading fun. Allow your child to pick books on subjects that interest her or him.

4. Words are everywhere—not just in books. Practice reading signs, packages, and cereal boxes with your child.

5. Set a good example. Make sure your child sees YOU reading.

Why Green Light Readers Is the Best Series for Your New Reader

- Created exclusively for beginning readers by some of the biggest and brightest names in children's books

- Reinforces the reading skills your child is learning in school

- Encourages children to read—and finish—books by themselves

- Offers extra enrichment through fun, age-appropriate activities unique to each story

- Incorporates characteristics of the Reading Recovery program used by educators

- Developed with Harcourt School Publishers and credentialed educational consultants